This book belongs to

Colette, EMMA

Michelle, ALICÉ

Kalix

To Linda and John, for being
such nice neighbors
– CF

For Mik, with love
– GH

tiger tales
an imprint of ME Media, LLC
202 Old Ridgefield Road, Wilton, CT 06897
This edition published in the United States 2006
First published in the United States 2004
Originally published in Great Britain 2004 by Little Tiger Press
An imprint of Magi Publications
Text copyright © 2004 Claire Freedman
Illustrations copyright © 2004 Gaby Hansen
ISBN-13: 978-1-58925-398-8
ISBN-10: 1-58925-398-1
Printed in China
5 7 9 10 8 6

Library of Congress Cataloging-in-Publication Data

Freedman, Claire.
  Oops-a-Daisy! / by Claire Freedman ; illustrated by Gaby Hansen.
    p. cm.
Summary: As little Daisy Rabbit struggles to learn how to hop, her mother
points out other baby animals having trouble with their lessons until Daisy
realizes that everyone needs practice when trying something new.
  ISBN 1-58925-037-0 (Hardcover)
  ISBN 1-58925-398-1 (Paperback)
 [1. Rabbits—Fiction. 2. Jumping—Fiction. 3. Babies—Fiction.
4. Perseverance (Ethics)—Fiction.] I. Hansen, Gaby, ill. II. Title.
PZ7.F87275 Oo 2004
[E]—dc22
                                                    2003015856

Oops-a-Daisy!

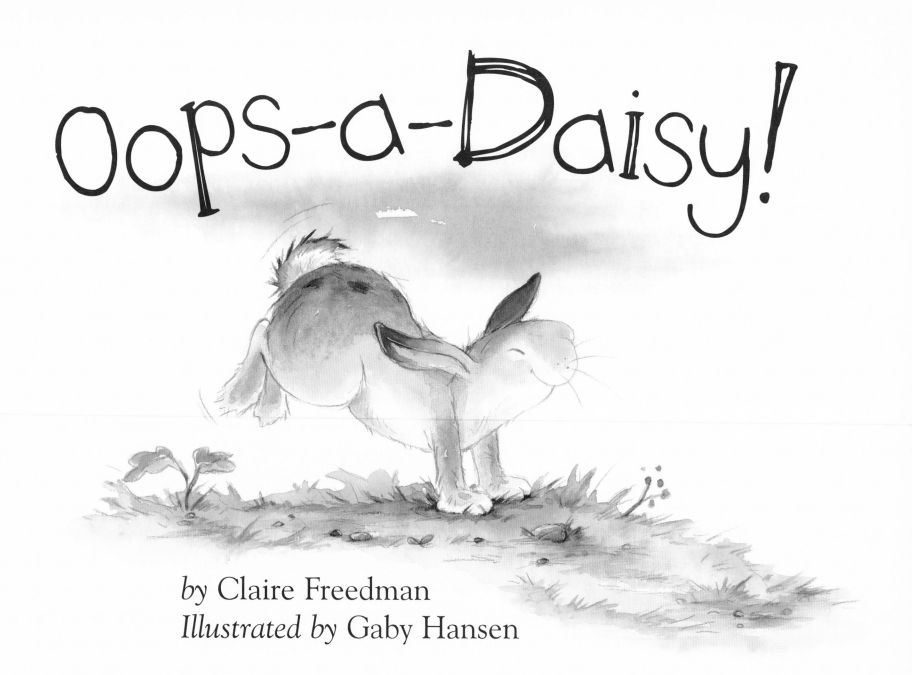

by Claire Freedman
Illustrated by Gaby Hansen

tiger tales

There was a lot of jumping and thumping over in the meadow. Mama Rabbit was teaching Daisy how to hop.

"I'm going to try hopping all by myself!" Daisy cried excitedly. "Watch me, Mama!"

Daisy took a huge leap, lost her balance, and fell over backward!

"Never mind!" said Mama Rabbit.
"Try again."
So Daisy did . . .

hippity-hoppity flop!

hoppity-floppity whoops!

"I don't think I can do it, Mama!"
Daisy cried.

"No one gets it right the first time,"
said Mama Rabbit, picking up Daisy
and dusting her off. "Look at Little
Mouse over by the duck pond."

Mama Mouse was showing Little Mouse
how to climb grass to reach the golden seeds
at the top.

Little Mouse inched closer and closer to the top. She had almost reached the seeds when . . .

slippity-flippity!

Little Mouse slid down again with a bump!
"Learning new things can be hard for
everyone!" Daisy said.

Daisy decided to practice little bunny hops.

"Stay in a straight line," Mama Rabbit called. "That's it!"

Up down, up down wobbled Daisy through the tall grass.

"Hooray, I can do it!" she cried. "Small hops are easier!"

Daisy saw a big molehill ahead. She jumped a huge jump...

whoopsity-oopsity!

"Ouch! Who put that
prickly thistle there?" Daisy
said. "And why won't my
feet do what I tell them to?"

"They will, in time!" said Mama.
She picked up Daisy and gave her
a hug. "Have you seen the mess
Little Badger is making?"

Little Badger was out in the field,
learning how to dig tunnels...

crashity-smashity!

Another one of his tunnels collapsed.
Little Badger and Daddy Badger were getting
muddier and muddier.

"I'm glad I'm not the only one who needs more practice,"
giggled Daisy.

Daisy and Mama Rabbit rested by the duck pond. Blue-green dragonflies darted around them whizzily-busily.

"Ribbit!" A big frog hopped out through the tall grass.

"I wish I could jump like that!" said Daisy. "Do you think I ever will?"

"You'll jump even higher!" Mama replied.

"Really?" cried Daisy, leaping up. "I'll try some more!"

"One, two . . . one, two," counted Daisy as she bounced. "Whee, look at me! Hopping is fun!"

"That's much better," Mama Rabbit called. "Oh no! Watch out, Daisy!" . . .

bumpity-thumpity!

Daisy slithered down the slippery
bank and skidded into the pond!
    "Ribbit, ribbit!" croaked the frog
in surprise.
    "Help!" Daisy cried. "I'm stuck
in the mud!"

Mama Rabbit ran down and
pulled Daisy free.

"I was so busy counting that I
didn't see the pond," sighed Daisy.
"There's so much to remember
all at once!"

"Cheer up, Daisy," Mama Rabbit
said. "Let's practice together." Paw in
paw, Daisy and Mama Rabbit hopped
and skipped around the duck pond.

Little Duckling was out on the water, practicing his swimming.

"Little Duckling isn't doing very well," said Daisy. "He can only swim in tiny circles!"

Then suddenly...

splashity-crashity!

Little Duckling sailed right into some
water lilies! Quickly his mother swam across
to untangle him.

"There's someone else who didn't look
where they were going!" Mama Rabbit smiled.

Daisy laughed. "I'm going to try hopping
by myself one more time!" she said.

Up down, up down bounced Daisy.
Wibbly-wobbly, hippity-hoppity hop!
  "That's it!" cried Mama. "Keep going!"
  "Did you see how high I jumped?" called Daisy proudly.
"I was almost flying! I can do it, Mama! I can do it!"
  "Well done, Daisy!" said Mama Rabbit. "You're hopping!"

Daisy hopped . . .

and skipped . . .

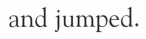

and jumped.

At last her legs were too tired to keep hopping!

"I'll have to carry you home this evening!" Mama laughed.

Happily, Daisy climbed into Mama Rabbit's arms and buried herself snuggly-huggly into her soft warm fur.

"Do you think Little Mouse, Little Badger, and Little Duckling learned how to climb and dig and swim?" Daisy asked Mama sleepily.

"I'm sure they did!" Mama
Rabbit whispered. "In the end!"

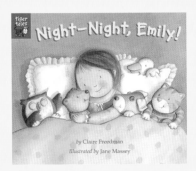

Night-Night, Emily!
by Claire Freedman
illustrated by Jane Massey
ISBN 1-58925-390-6

Where There's A Bear, There's Trouble!
by Michael Catchpool
illustrated by Vanessa Cabban
ISBN 1-58925-389-2

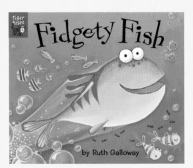

Fidgety Fish
by Ruth Galloway
ISBN 1-58925-377-9

Snarlyhissopus
by Alan MacDonald
illustrated by Louise Voce
ISBN 1-58975-370-1

Explore the world of tiger tales!

More fun-filled and exciting stories await you!
Look for these titles and more at your local library or bookstore.
And have fun reading!

tiger tales

202 Old Ridgefield Road, Wilton, CT 06897

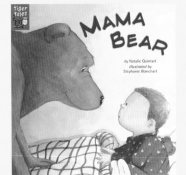

Mama Bear
by Natalie Quintart
illustrated by Stéphanie Blanchart
ISBN 1-58925-394-9

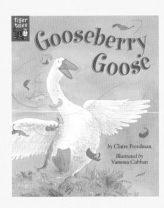

Gooseberry Goose
by Claire Freedman
illustrated by Vanessa Cabban
ISBN 1-58925-392-2

**The Von Hamm Family:
Alex and the Tart**
by Guido van Genechten
ISBN 1-58925-393-0

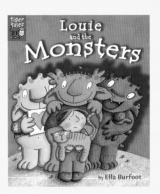

Louie and the Monsters
by Ella Burfoot
ISBN 1-58925-395-7